When 10-year-old Ben Tennyson stumbles upon a mysterious alien device in the woods one summer, little does he realise that his life is set to change - forever.

As soon as the watch-like Omnitrix quite literally gets a grip on him, Ben discovers it gives him the ability to transform into 10 different alien super-beings, each one with awesome powers!

Using the Omnitrix to cause super-powered mischief turns out to be fun, but will Ben learn to use his might to fight for good?

*READ ON AND FIND OUT . . .*

**EGMONT**
*We bring stories to life*

Published in Great Britain 2009
by Egmont UK Limited
239 Kensington High Street, London W8 6SA

Ben 10 and all related characters and elements
are trademarks of and © Cartoon Network.
(s09)

Adapted from the animated series by
Barry Hutchison

1 3 5 7 9 10 8 6 4 2

A CIP catalogue record for this title is available from
the British Library

Printed and bound in Great Britain by the CPI Group

All rights reserved. No part of this publication may be
reproduced, stored in a retrieval system, or transmitted, in any
form or by any means, electronic, mechanical, photocopying,
recording or otherwise, without the prior permission of the
publisher and copyright owner.

## CHAPTER ONE

# A FIRE FLY SQUEEEEAK!

**B**en dragged his nose across a side window of The Rust Bucket, leaving a sticky trail of snot. Then he puffed out his cheeks, pressed his lips to the glass and crossed his eyes. It made him look like the world's ugliest fish.

In the next lane of the busy motorway, a boy of around Ben's age looked on, laughing. He was sitting in the back seat of his dad's car, and he and Ben were locked in battle.

The boy hooked his fingers in the corners of his mouth and pulled, waggling his tongue around like a snake. It was a scary-face duel, and right now both boys were evenly matched.

From her seat on the other side of The Rust Bucket, Gwen looked over at her cousin and sighed.

'I'd warn you that you face might freeze like that,' she said, 'but in your case it would be an improvement.'

Ben ignored her. He was too focused on what was happening in the other car. His opponent had turned his back and was frantically chewing on something. Ben had a good idea what was coming next.

The boy in the car spun in his seat and opened his mouth wide. A soggy mush of chewed-up cheeseburger sat perched on the end of his tongue.

'Oh, man! The "see-food special"!' Ben groaned. He knew there was only one way he could hope to win the battle now. He ducked down out of sight and twisted the control dial on the Omnitrix. 'Time to pull out the secret weapon.'

Over in the other car, the boy swallowed his food and waited. He was confident of victory. There weren't many moves that could rival the see-food special for sheer grossness. The duel was as good as won.

### SPLAT!

A wad of icky green goo hit the inside of The Rust Bucket's window. A hideous, insect-like face appeared behind the glass, green ooze dripping from its antennae. Ben had transformed into the alien he called Stinkfly!

A scream of fright burst from the boy's mouth. At the front of the vehicle, his dad turned to see what was going on. His eyes grew wide as he caught sight of the giant insect and he screamed too, pushing the accelerator pedal to the floor. The car raced off along the motorway.

Stinkfly collapsed on the motorhome floor, giggling uncontrollably. Gwen stood over him, shaking her head.

'There is such a thing as taking a joke too far, you know.' She scowled as she went to sit down then cried out in shock when she sat in a splodge of smelly alien slime.

At that, Stinkfly erupted into even louder laughter. 'Impossible!' he cried. 'Funny is funny!'

'Ben, better get up here.' Grandpa's voice sounded serious. Something had to be wrong.

With a screech of brakes, The Rust Bucket came to a sudden stop. Stinkfly slid along the floor then tumbled clumsily into the driver's cabin, right next to Grandpa Max.

'Oh, good.' Grandpa Max nodded. 'You're all ready to go. We got trouble ahead.'

Grandpa, Gwen and Stinkfly all stared out at the twisted tangle of metal that was blocking the road a few hundred metres away. A truck and a fuel tanker had crashed and now flames were licking the sides of both vehicles.

Inside the cab of the truck, they could just make out the shape of the driver. He was

kicking and hammering against the doors but they were jammed shut. He was trapped!

'If that fuel catches fire,' began Grandpa, 'that truck will become a rocket to the moon.'

Stinkfly didn't need to be told what to do next. He kicked open the door of The Rust Bucket and launched himself towards the flaming wreckage. Grandpa and Gwen jumped down behind him and set about keeping the gathering crowd of onlookers out of harm's way.

The heat from the fire was blistering. Even with all his alien power, Stinkfly struggled to get close enough to pull the driver free. He made a dive for a gap in the flames but the space closed over, crackling and spitting as the fire burned hotter.

'The fire's too intense. I wish I was Heatblast,' he muttered. A thought suddenly struck him. 'Hey, that gives me an idea.'

Stinkfly's wings buzzed, carrying him up above the flames. Thick clouds of black smoke swirled around him, making it hard to see. The fuel in the tanker must be getting dangerously hot by now. He would only have one chance at this, so his plan had to work.

**SPU-LAT!**

A thick ball of green goo spat from one of Stinkfly's antennae. It splattered down on to a burning chunk of metal. The slime smothered the flames, snuffing them out completely.

**SPU-LAT!**
**SPU-LAT!**
**SPU-LAT!**

More dollops of stinky sludge rained down on the fire, coating the wreckage and the ground in a thick layer of slippery green gloop.

Inside the truck, the driver was still panicking. One minute he'd been watching the fire rage closer, the next all the windows had been covered with . . . something horrible. Now the glass was all sludgy, everything was dark and he had no idea what was going on.

A screech of tearing metal made him jump. He looked up to see a pair of curved claws rip clean through the roof of the cab. The roof was torn away, and the driver found himself staring at the biggest, ugliest bug he had ever seen in his life.

Four insect-like arms caught the driver by the shoulders and Stinkfly launched into the air.

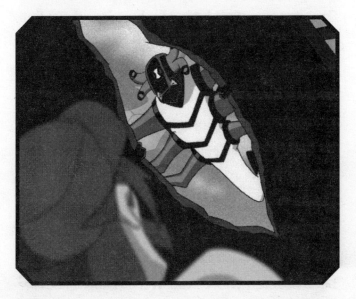

He swooped down over the road, admiring the splodges of sticky green.

'Loogies save lives,' he said with a smile, placing the driver safely back on the ground.

'Aaah!' came a scream from the crowd of onlookers. Stinkfly turned to see the boy from the car pointing at him.

Grandpa Max frowned. He turned his gaze on Stinkfly and narrowed his eyes suspiciously. Stinkfly swallowed nervously. Grandpa wouldn't be happy if he found out Ben had used the Omnitrix to win a face-pulling contest.

'Wow, look at the time,' Stinkfly said, buzzing up into the air. 'Gotta fly!'

※ ※ ※

A few hours later, Ben sat in the front passenger seat of The Rust Bucket, watching the barren landscape trundle slowly by. His grandpa hummed quietly to himself as he drove. Behind them both, Gwen sat at the motorhome's table reading a large road sign.

'You'll have a ball with It,' she read. 'Next exit.'

'Come on, Grandpa,' Ben pleaded. 'At least give us a hint of what It is.'

Grandpa shook his head and smirked. 'No hints. I've been planning this stop all summer.' He guided the motorhome on to the motorway exit ramp, before bringing it to a stop by the side of the road.

'Now,' said Grandpa, opening his door, 'both of you close your eyes.'

The cousins did as they were told. Grandpa skipped excitedly round to the other side of The Rust Bucket and pulled open the door. He took both children by the hand and led them out.

'OK, open them up,' he grinned.

Ben and Gwen opened their eyes. Before them stood a collection of buildings. They were all painted with bright colours, but the paint was faded and the whole place looked as if it had seen better days.

On top of a handful of the buildings were some giant novelty props. A ten-metre-long hot dog sat on one low roof. A huge glass bowl was perched on another. There was even an enormous antelope's head sticking up from the roof of a dingy motel. As far as Ben was concerned, lame didn't even begin to describe the place.

'Ta-da!' cried Grandpa, grinning from ear to ear. He pointed up to a tall sign made of bright neon lights and read it aloud: 'Welcome to Sparksville!'

## CHAPTER TWO

## IT

**G**randpa bounced on the spot like an excited puppy. 'Is this place great or what?'

Ben looked around at the faded paintwork of the nearest buildings. 'Uh . . . I'll go with "or what".'

'Come on, what's more exciting than the world's biggest fish bowl?'

Ben thought about this for a second. 'Everything?'

A tall skinny man in a badly fitting suit shuffled over to join the group. His hair was greasy and matted against his head. A mess of stubble covered his chin.

'As the Mayor of Sparksville, I welcome

you, O, seekers of wonder,' he drawled. The effort of speaking seemed to drain the man's energy. He gave Grandpa Max the briefest of nods then slowly shuffled back the way he'd come.

Once the mayor had left, Grandpa turned to his grandchildren. 'I know you guys are probably excited to see It,' he said, pressing two tickets into Ben's hand, 'so I'll go check us in.'

Ben and Gwen watched him scamper off towards the motel. They looked at each other, shook their heads, then started along the street to where a sign promised some 'Exciting Exhibits'.

They eventually arrived at a lopsided wooden ticket booth. A turnstile gate sat next to it. Beyond the turnstile, a narrow doorway led through to an area surrounded by a tall fence. Like the rest of Sparksville, the booth seemed to be deserted.

**DING!**

Ben rang the bell on the desk. At first nothing happened, but after several seconds a familiar figure stepped through the doorway.

'Tickets, please,' droned the man.

'I thought you were the mayor?' said Ben with a frown.

The man took their tickets, tore them in half, then handed one half back. 'He who wears the crown is burdened by many hats, son,' he said.

Ben tried to think of a reply, but quickly decided it wasn't worth the effort. With Gwen following behind, he pushed through the turnstile and into the exhibition area.

The exhibits were even less impressive than Ben and Gwen had expected. There was a robotic jackalope: a mythical creature with the body of a rabbit and the horns of an antelope. The one on display had a set of antlers missing. Its mouth made a mechanical whir as it chomped endlessly on a large cardboard carrot.

The World's Biggest House of Cards exhibit was not what the name suggested either. The cousins had imagined a carefully arranged stack of thousands of playing cards, all forming the shape of a house. Instead what they found were seven extremely large playing cards, stacked up to form a sort of triangle shape that wobbled as they walked past.

The other exhibits were just as bad. The world's biggest fish bowl was just a really large – and completely empty – glass bowl. The enormous hot dog they'd seen from outside turned out to be just a billboard for a shop selling overpriced snack versions.

Finally, they arrived at a tall building that looked like an old barn. Painted on the barn in metre-high letters were two short words: IT'S HERE. The mayor shuffled up to join them as Ben and Gwen approached the entrance.

'Through these doors lies the weirdest, wildest thing ever to find its way to Sparksville,' he announced, his voice as flat and emotionless as ever.

**CREEEEAK!**

The twin doors to the barn swung inwards, revealing nothing but darkness.

'Please tell me this is It,' Ben sighed, leading his cousin inside. 'Because I can't stand It any more.'

As they walked through the darkness, several signs began to illuminate on the walls on either side of the path.

'Do not touch It,' Ben read.

'Do not photograph It,' said Gwen as another sign blinked into life beside her.

'Do not use batteries or electrical equipment anywhere near It,' Ben continued. He had to admit, whatever It was, it was starting to sound almost interesting.

A second later, he realised he could not have been more wrong.

'This is It?' he snorted as they arrived at

a wide, looming shape. Gwen stared up at the object, her mouth hanging open.

'It's a big ball of rubber bands,' she said, at last.

The mayor appeared behind them. 'And who knows what secrets lie within?' he said.

'Uh, more rubber bands?' suggested Ben.

'Stay as long as you like,' the mayor told them, backing out of the barn. 'Mind the signs.'

Ben barely waited for him to leave before turning to Gwen. 'Look at this place!' he complained. 'These guys are full of It. We've been punked.'

'It is pretty lame,' Gwen admitted. 'I can't believe Grandpa was so excited about this place.' She spotted a mischievous expression creep across Ben's face. 'I know that look,' she said. 'What are you planning?'

Without a word, Ben slammed his hand down on the Omnitrix. A swirl of green energy wrapped itself around him. When it cleared, he had transformed into the powerful red-skinned alien, Four Arms.

Without any effort, Four Arms scooped up the rubber-band ball and began bouncing it like a basketball.

'One good prank deserves another,' he said, his eyes sparkling.

Gwen smirked. 'For once, I agree with you. Got something special in mind?'

'I dunno,' shrugged the alien. He held the
ball next to where his nose would be if he had
one. 'Maybe the world's biggest booger?'

He flicked the ball up into the air and
balanced it on his shoulders. It wobbled back
and forth unsteadily.

'Careful, dweeb. You'll drop it,' Gwen
warned.

'Not a chance,' Four Arms replied. He
caught the ball with one hand and held it
above his head. 'I could lift this thing with

three arms tied behind my –'

The ball rolled off the alien's hand before he could even finish the sentence. It boinged once on the dusty floor then shot upwards, smashing through the flimsy barn roof with a deafening **KER-ASH!**

Four Arms looked up at the gaping hole in the roof and winced. 'Oops.'

※ ※ ※

Outside, the rubber ball bounced off on a path of destruction. It crashed down on the gift shop then rebounded away, smashing the giant hot dog to pieces. Several more exhibits found themselves squashed, shattered or smashed before the ball finally came to rest among the ruins of the house of cards.

Four Arms and Gwen rushed over to check out the damage. Things were pretty bad. Half of the exhibits were broken.

As Four Arms began to pick up the fallen cards, Gwen slapped him hard across the back of the head.

'Ow! What was that for?' he demanded.

'For turning me into a criminal,' Gwen snapped.

The alien flashed her a smile. 'Don't get your shorts in a twist. I'll just put everything back the way it was. No problem.'

As he gripped the ball with his powerful hands, the Omnitrix gave a sudden bleep. In a flash of blinding red light, Four Arms transformed back into Ben.

'OK,' Ben gulped. 'Maybe a little problem.'

The cousins were so busy worrying about what they should do next that neither one noticed the strange sparks of red energy crackling across the surface of the Omnitrix. They flashed like tiny bolts of lightning, before being drawn into the rubber-band ball.

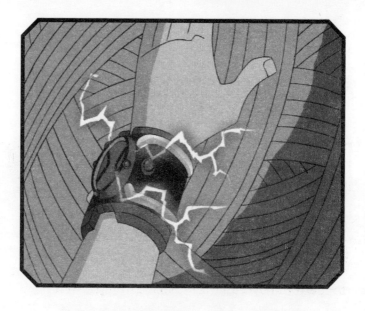

At that very moment, deep inside the ball, something slowly began to stir . . .

## CHAPTER THREE

# WHAT'S A MEGAWHATT?

*G*randpa Max had checked them all into the Sideways Motel: the only place to stay in town. Like everywhere else in Sparksville, the motel had a theme, and the clue to this particular theme was in the title.

Ben and Gwen stared down at the door to their room. It was mounted sideways on the wall, meaning they would have to crawl on their hands and knees to get through it.

'What are we going to tell Grandpa?' Gwen fretted as she and Ben kneeled on the floor.

'Nothing,' replied Ben. 'We just play dumb.'

'Easy for you. You're a lot better at it than

I am,' Gwen snorted. She turned the handle of the door, pushed it open and crawled inside.

'Hey, there you are!' cried Grandpa Max as Gwen and Ben clambered through.

The inside of the room was mind-boggling. One wall was covered in carpet. Tables and chairs were attached to it, giving the impression the whole room had been tipped on to its side. Even the beds were stuck to the carpeted wall. Ben couldn't begin to imagine how they were supposed to sleep in them.

Grandpa stood in the middle of the room, smiling broadly. The floor beneath his feet was covered in patterned wallpaper. The Sideways Motel really lived up to its name.

'Isn't this place a riot?' Grandpa grinned.

'Why? What'd you see?' yelped Gwen. 'We don't know anything about it!'

Ben stepped in front of his cousin and gave her a nudge with his elbow. 'She means it's great, Grandpa,' he said, smiling. His eyes flicked to the crazy wall-mounted furniture. 'Can't wait to check out the bathroom.'

�֎ ✻ ✻

Over at the house of cards, the surface of the rubber-band ball was beginning to shudder and shake. A coil of yellow electrical energy snaked out through the rubber and arced through the air until it found the overhead power cables.

Boosted in strength, the energy crackled and fizzed along them. Large sparks shot off in all directions, scorching the exhibits closest to it. One long tendril of electricity zapped through the air, burning a hole clean through the town's welcome sign.

**POP!**

A short, stubby black-and-yellow shape squeezed free of the rubber-band ball and took in the damage he had caused. Energy buzzed behind the creature's eyes as it threw back its head and laughed. He had been imprisoned for too long, weakened and trapped. Not any more. At last his ordeal was over. At last his powers were returning.

At last he was free.

The morning sunlight streamed in through the window of the sideways bedroom. Ben and

Gwen shifted carefully in their wall-mounted beds as they slowly woke up.

It had been a long night. First of all, it had taken nearly an hour just to get into the beds, and then another twenty minutes had been wasted wrapping the covers tightly around them so they wouldn't fall out. In the end, they had slept tangled in the covers, using them like hammocks. It wasn't comfortable by a long shot.

'What the heck happened here?' Grandpa's voice jolted the cousins awake. They both slipped from the beds and hit the floor with a bump.

'Argh! He knows everything! We are so busted,' said Gwen in a panicked whisper. 'We have to come clean.'

Ben shook his head. 'Sometimes it's hard to believe you're really a kid. Never admit anything until you absolutely have to. Got it?'

The door to the room swung inwards and Grandpa Max poked his head through.

'Benjamin. Gwendolyn. Get out here,' he barked.

'"Gwendolyn"?' gulped Gwen. 'We're doomed.'

✖ ✖ ✖

After hurriedly getting dressed, Ben and Gwen joined their grandpa and the handful of other tourists on the main street. Their eyes grew wide as they spotted the destruction. Every exhibit, stand and shop front was either smashed or smoking. Or both. The damage Ben had caused as Four Arms had been nowhere near as bad as this.

'Whoa! What happened?' asked Ben.

'I don't know,' Max told him. 'Looks like a tornado tore through here overnight.'

Ben smiled. They were off the hook. 'Good,' he said. 'Uh, I mean, yeah. It was just one of those freaky nature things. Right, Gwen?'

The mayor stepped up to join them. His face was even more serious than usual.

'I think it's pretty clear who's responsible for these juvenile acts,' he droned.

'"Juvenile acts"?' repeated Grandpa. He turned his gaze on Ben and Gwen. 'If I didn't know better, that sounds like –'

'Oh, I'm not talkin' about these youngsters,' interrupted the mayor.

Grandpa, Ben and Gwen all raised their eyebrows in surprise. 'You're not?' they all asked at once.

'Yeah, well, if they didn't do it, who did?' asked Grandpa Max.

Suddenly, a bolt of electrical energy whizzed past Grandpa's ear. He turned to find the small black-and-yellow creature sitting on his shoulder, smiling at him.

Before he could react, the creature zapped away. It appeared on the ground beside Ben for just long enough to kick him in the shins then

leaped on to Gwen's back. She twisted, trying to shake the giggling gremlin off, but it yanked the back of her T-shirt up over her head and quickly zoomed away.

'What . . . was that?' gasped Ben.

'Megawhatt,' drawled the mayor.

'Mega what?'

'Exactly.' The mayor nodded. 'Normally wrapped up tight inside of It. That is, until last night.'

Ben and Gwen exchanged a guilty glance,

but said nothing. Instead, they turned their attention to the Megawhatt. It was speeding around the town, yanking down the trousers of a few tourists, messing up the hair of others and generally being a nuisance.

'Some say it might be a ball of lightning come alive,' the mayor said. 'Others think it's static cling run amok. Tough to say.'

'Maybe it's an alien,' suggested Gwen.

The mayor rolled his eyes. 'Alien? That's

just plain kooky talk.'

They watched the little creature clamber inside a drinks vending machine. Almost at once, electrical energy began to fizz across the machine's surface.

'What's it doing?' asked Ben with a frown.

'It eats electricity. The more it gobbles, the more powerful it gets.'

## PTCHOOW!

A soft-drink can exploded from the machine's dispenser. It rocketed towards the group, missing Ben's head by millimetres. Another one shot out just behind it, then another, and another, the cans hurtling through the air like cannonballs.

'It's also got a dangerous sense of humour,' the mayor continued as they all took cover behind the broken remains of the jackalope exhibit.

'You left that thing inside a rubber-band ball all this time?' asked Grandpa Max. 'Wasn't that kind of dangerous?'

'Not so long as people minded the signs,' sighed the mayor.

Ben bit his lip. He knew the words were going to come out, but he fought to hold them back. 'All right, we did it! We're guilty,' he cried.

'So much for admit nothing,' muttered Gwen.

Grandpa Max glared at both of them. 'We're going to talk about this later,' he said. 'But for now how do we stop this thing, Mr Mayor?'

The mayor shrugged. 'Whatcha mean "we"?' he said, taking a seat on a nearby bench. 'You let it out. You catch it.'

## CHAPTER FOUR

# THE APPLIANCE OF SCIENCE

**B**en, Gwen and Grandpa walked slowly along the near-deserted main street. Their eyes were peeled for any sign of the Megawhatt, but so far the mischievous little creature was staying hidden.

'Should we try to lure it out with some batteries or something?' asked Gwen.

Grandpa opened his mouth to reply, but a sudden surge of electricity shooting up his trouser leg silenced him. He yelped with shock as the Megawhatt caught hold of his underwear and lifted him off the ground. Grandpa hung there in mid-air, caught in an atomic wedgie.

'That's not funny,' he groaned. 'It's just painful.'

'Don't worry, Grandpa,' said Ben, twisting the dial of the Omnitrix. 'I know just the hero to deal with a troublemaker like this!'

**SLAM!**

Ben's hand slapped down on the watch and the familiar swirl of energy wrapped around him. When it cleared, the shape-shifting Upgrade stood in Ben's place.

'Why go Upgrade?' asked Gwen, puzzled.

'It's complicated. You wouldn't understand.'

Gwen smirked. 'The watch didn't let you change into what you wanted to, did it?'

Upgrade hesitated for a moment. 'Shut up,' he muttered at last.

Meanwhile, the Megawhatt had dropped Grandpa and was zipping off to cause more mayhem. He zoomed up to where a giant ketchup bottle stood on top the restaurant roof.

His electrical energy flashed across the bottle's surface and suddenly the 'ketchup' inside began to boil. The sticky red liquid exploded upwards like lava from a volcano before raining down on the street below.

'OK, twinkle toes, time to go home!'

The Megawhatt looked down to see the rubber-band ball trundling along the road – and Upgrade was running on top of it, moving it forwards!

**TWANG!**

As the ball rolled over a chunk of debris, one of the giant bands snapped. It pinged through the air at supersonic speed. With a crack, it punched a hole clean through a car windscreen.

Several more bands sprung free. The small groups of worried tourists who were gathered on the street had to throw themselves to the ground to avoid being hit by the elastic missiles.

'Hey, doofus, whose side are you on?' cried Gwen.

Over on the bench, the mayor was munching on popcorn and watching the show. 'Is it just me,' he mumbled to no one in particular, 'or is there a lot of excitement today?'

Upgrade jumped down from the rubber-band ball, scared of doing any more damage. The Megawhatt floated out of reach above him. It giggled uncontrollably, delighted by all the extra destruction.

Upgrade scowled angrily. As he did, a powerful beam of green energy erupted from his single eye. It streaked towards the Megawhatt, who had to twist at the last moment to avoid being zapped.

'Whoa, that's new!' Upgrade gasped. He pointed up at the floating troublemaker. 'Not so funny now, is it?'

The Megawhatt disagreed. Exploding into another fit of giggles, he began twisting and weaving around the alien hero, ducking out of reach whenever Upgrade got too close.

Then, with one desperate leap, Upgrade's hands wrapped round the Megawhatt's tiny body. He held the creature up triumphantly before a blast of electrical energy forced him to release his grip.

'OK,' Upgrade groaned, his whole body shaking. 'Do not touch the electrical guy when you're made of living metal.'

Grandpa and Gwen stood nearby, watching the fight. They were worried. The Megawhatt was proving to be a tougher opponent than any of them had expected.

'How are we going to ground that electric devil?' Grandpa wondered.

Gwen clicked her fingers. 'Grandpa, you're a genius!'

'Well, thank you, Gwen.' Grandpa Max smiled. He paused for a moment before asking, 'Why?'

Upgrade darted past, pursued by dozens of mini lightning bolts. He bobbed and ducked, avoiding most of them, but a single bolt hit him on the behind with a loud hiss.

'That's it,' he growled. 'I'm pulling the plug on this guy's pranks.'

Reaching down, he tore a heavy iron manhole cover free of the ground. Taking aim, he launched the cover like a discus. It made a low **WHUM** sound as it hurtled through the air. By the time the Megawhatt spotted it, it was too late. The manhole cover sliced through him, cutting him in half straight down the middle.

For a moment, the two halves of the creature hung there, suspended in mid-air. Then, to Upgrade's horror, they became two wholes! The two Megawhatts looked at each other and began to giggle with uncontrolled glee.

'OK, so that wasn't the best idea,' admitted Upgrade. He looked down as the

Omnitrix began to flash red. With a bleep the watch timed out, forcing the alien back into human form.

Lightning struck the ground on either side of Ben, melting the tarmac and spraying him with sharp shards of hot stone. Throwing his hands over his head for protection, he sprinted away, searching for somewhere to hide.

Ben almost screamed as he ran round a corner and straight into the path of an oncoming truck. The vehicle's brakes squealed sharply and the passenger door swung open. With the Megawhatts closing fast, Ben hopped up into the cab and pulled the door closed behind him.

In the driver's seat, Grandpa Max crunched the truck into gear and began to drive. Gwen slid over in her seat to make room for Ben to sit.

'Grandpa, what are you doing?' panted Ben.

Grandpa Max jabbed a thumb out of the back window of the cab. Ben turned to see a giant thermometer – one of Sparksville's exhibits – strapped to the back of the flatbed. 'Giving these sparklers a science lesson they won't forget,' Grandpa said with a grin.

The Megawhatts chittered excitedly as they sliced through the air behind the truck. The thermometer was one of the few exhibits they hadn't yet destroyed, and they were determined they would smash it to pieces too.

Gwen watched them in the truck's

rear-view mirror. Her hand slipped down on to a control lever. 'Hey, Mega-wierds,' she cried, yanking the lever sharply, 'come get us!'

The back of the truck began to lift. With a groan of metal, the thermometer slipped from the flatbed and speared itself into the ground. The Megawhatts were moving too fast to stop. They smacked into the side of the thermometer, and – with a bright flash – vanished into it.

The truck trundled to a stop and the three heroes leaped out.

'What happened?' asked Ben.

'Just used the biggest thermometer as a lightning rod,' said Gwen proudly. 'Who needs an alien superhero when you've got good old-fashioned brain power?'

A quiet cough from behind them caught their attention. They turned to find the mayor standing there, still munching on his popcorn. 'Course,' he began, 'the ground's basically just one big conductor.'

Ben frowned. 'What does that mean?'

Gwen's jaw dropped open as she realised what she had done. This was bad. This was really bad.

'It means the Megawhatts are just zipping around underground until they find some way to get back to the surface.'

## BRRRRRRING BRRRRRRING!

As if on cue, the phone in the closest payphone booth began to ring. A second later, more joined the chorus. In no time at all it sounded as though every phone in the town were ringing at once.

'They're in the underground phone lines,' Grandpa muttered, just as sparks began to emerge from the telephones' handsets.

Ben and Gwen gasped as hundreds upon hundreds of tiny Megawhatts spewed out from inside the telephones and crackled across the sky.

## CHAPTER FIVE

# PRANKED

**G**wen watched, horrified, as the army of Megawhatts set about destroying what was left of Sparksville. Even without looking, she could feel her cousin's stare.

'Ben Tennyson, don't say a word,' she sighed.

'Hey, I'm just glad I wasn't the one who screwed up this time,' Ben said with a grin.

A swarm of the energy creatures swooped past them. They settled on top of the giant hot-dog display. In just a few seconds, they had chomped all the way through it. They patted their swollen bellies then began to snigger.

**BUUUUUUURP!**

The belch was so loud it shattered all the windows along the main street. High on top of a nearby towering building, a glass display case also exploded into shards. Thirty or more metre-long spikes of wood fell like javelins towards the ground, narrowly missing a gathering crowd of onlookers.

As the tourists ran for safety, the mayor picked up another handful of popcorn and shook his head sadly. 'There goes the world's largest collection of toothpicks,' he said. 'Oh, the humanity.'

Grandpa Max led the tourists out of harm's way then returned to join his grandchildren. 'Those creeps' idea of good clean fun is going to have us all pushing up daisies.'

Gwen spun to face her cousin. 'Don't just stand there, doofus. Dial up some help!'

Ben held up the Omnitrix. The display was still red, which meant it hadn't yet recharged. 'Duh! Like I haven't been trying.' He glanced along the street. The Megawhatts were nowhere to be seen. 'Ah . . . where'd they go?'

Grandpa Max narrowed his eyes suspiciously. 'I don't know,' he confessed. 'But I don't think it's good.'

**KA-BOOM!**

The ground beneath them shook violently. The wall of the planetarium building crumbled and a towering robotic monster appeared. Its head, hands and feet were all made from the planets of the solar system – or models of them, at least. The rest of its enormous frame was formed from bent and buckled chunks of machinery. As it clanked along the street towards the main highway, sparks of yellow energy spat from its mechanical joints.

'Well, there's something you don't see every day,' said Grandpa, whistling under his breath. 'Come on,' he urged, running for The Rust Bucket, 'we'll head it off in the –'

He stopped and stared. His beloved

motorhome was a mess: every one of its wheels had been removed and bright green graffiti was painted all along one side.

'"U am lame",' read Ben. 'That's weak.'

'And don't even get me started on the grammar and the spelling,' Gwen said, scowling.

'I reckon they'll head for the big hydroelectric dam to power up,' droned the mayor as he finished the last of his popcorn. 'After that, they'll just wipe out the next town and so on and so on.

'They think it's funny,' he continued. 'Megawhatts have got a real twisted sense of humour.'

A short distance away, sunlight glinted off the only glass object not to have been shattered by the Megawhatts' belch. Ben and Gwen both looked up at it and smiled.

'You thinking what I'm thinking?' asked Gwen.

'Yeah,' said Ben as the Omnitrix flicked back to green. 'Beat those pranksters at their own game.'

The planetarium robot drove its fists against the thick walls of the dam. Cracks began to appear in the rock, small at first, but becoming wider with each thundering punch.

## WHOOOSH!

A column of flame suddenly engulfed the mechanoid, driving it away from the dam wall. As the flame died, the robot looked up. The alien hero, Heatblast, stood on the top of the dam smiling down.

'This is your only warning,' Heatblast yelled. 'Knock off the funny business or I'll fry your twinkling butts!'

Swinging wildly, the planet creature smashed both fists against the dam, shaking it. Heatblast wobbled around, struggling to keep his balance, but it was no use. The alien slipped and began tumbling towards the ground.

Twisting in mid-air as he fell, Heatblast produced a blast of searing heat beneath his feet. He rode the flame trail down, banking at the last minute to avoid crashing down on to the concrete floor of the dam.

Soaring upwards, Heatblast reached the top of the dam just as the robot clambered up. It clanked towards the equipment used to store the energy produced by the dam. Heatblast had to stop it before it could reach the machinery or it would be too powerful to contain.

Turning sharply, the alien tried to close in on the Megawhatt-powered mechanoid, but he couldn't slow himself down enough to make the turn. With a crash he struck the top of the dam before bouncing to a painful stop right in the robot's path.

A planet-Mars-shaped foot lashed out and caught the fallen alien under the jaw. Heatblast was flipped backwards, over and over, until he eventually smashed hard against a solid brick wall.

The robot's mechanical components whirred as it advanced on the alien. Just before it reached its target, Gwen stepped in front of it. She held the end of a hose in her hands.

'You guys are all wet.' She smirked, giving the nozzle a twist. A spray of water hit the mechanoid in the face. It staggered backwards, thrashing with its arms as it tried to drive Gwen away.

'What's the matter?' growled Heatblast, back on his feet with a huge fireball forming between his hands. 'Can't take a joke?'

The robot couldn't get out of the way in time. The ball of fire exploded around it, so hot it melted the metal into silver liquid.

The Megawhatts weren't laughing as they swarmed from the wreckage of their creation. They chittered angrily and zapped through the air towards Heatblast. A cloud of choking black smoke suddenly sprang up and the Megawhatts began to cough and splutter. They thrashed around inside the smoke, but their enemy was nowhere to be found.

'Missed me, doofus!' cried a voice from somewhere above them. The Megawhatts floated up to find Heatblast standing on the roof of the dam's control room. A large object stood behind him, covered by an even larger sheet.

Blowing the creatures a kiss, Heatblast ducked beneath the sheet. Furious, the Megawhatts dived after him, their electrical bodies passing easily through the fabric.

From behind the covered object, Grandpa Max gave a cheer. 'Ben did it! They took the bait!'

He and Gwen each caught a corner of the sheet and pulled it away, revealing the world's largest fish bowl. Heatblast stood beside it smiling happily. Inside the glass bowl, the Megawhatts hammered frantically against the glass.

With a blast of flame, Heatblast sealed the top, turning the fish bowl into a perfect sphere of thick glass. When he'd finished, he stuck out his tongue at the trapped creatures and laughed.

'Nice touch using the fish bowl,' Grandpa said. 'With non-conductive glass sealed up tight, Sparky and his pals won't be going anywhere.'

'Once again, science saves the day,' said Gwen.

The Omnitrix gave a bleep, transforming Heatblast back into plain old Ben once again.

'With a little help from science fiction,' her cousin added.

✖ ✖ ✖

Repairs had already begun on Sparksville by the next morning. As Ben, Gwen and Grandpa prepared to leave, they met the mayor. He was standing beside a new exhibit that had not yet been unveiled.

'You folks done right by us,' he said.

'I hope this adventure wasn't a big setback for Sparksville,' Grandpa Max replied.

'More like a giant step forward, what with our new attraction. Soon we'll be raking 'em in.' He pulled away the sheet covering the exhibit. The world's largest fish bowl had been transformed into the world's largest light bulb. It glowed brightly, even in the morning sun.

'It'll be a humdinger,' the mayor drawled. 'So long as folks mind the signs.'

He pointed to a warning sign mounted on the base of the light bulb. 'In case of emergency,' Ben read, 'do not break the glass.'

After saying their goodbyes, the three heroes made their way back to The Rust Bucket. 'I think I'm pranked out for a while,' Ben admitted.

Grandpa nodded and stepped aside, letting Ben go before him into the motorhome. 'There is a time and a place for a practical joke,' he said as Ben began to pull open the door.

## SPLAAASH!

A bucket of ice-cold water that had been balancing on the door toppled, spilling its contents over Ben's head. Grandpa and Gwen both began to laugh.

'But funny is funny,' chuckled Grandpa. 'Especially when it's not on you!'

# BEN 10 BOOK COLLECTION

## HAVE YOU SEEN THEM ALL?

| | |
|---|---|
| **Ben 10 Alien Force Annual 2010** | 978 1 4052 4653 8; £7.99 |
| **Ben 10 Alien Force colour storybook 1 (Ben 10 Returns Part 1/Part 2)** | 978 1 4052 4799 3; £4.99 |
| **Ben 10 Alien Force colour storybook 2 (The Gauntlet/Be-Knighted)** | 978 1 4052 4800 6; £4.99 |
| **Ben 10 Amazing 3D Hero Vision** | 978 1 4052 4413 8; £3.99 |
| **Ben 10 Puzzle and Quiz Book** | 978 1 4052 4492 3; £3.99 |
| **Ben 10 Magnet Book** | 978 1 4052 4599 9; £5.99 |
| **Ben 10 All Action Stories & Flicker Book** | 978 1 4052 4512 8; £4.99 |
| **Ben 10 comic book 1 (And Then There Were 10)** | 978 1 4052 4663 7; £4.99 |
| **Ben 10 comic book 2 (Washington B.C.)** | 978 1 4052 4664 4; £4.99 |
| **Ben 10 comic book 3 (The Krakken)** | 978 1 4052 4804 4; £4.99 |

**Ben 10 comic book 4**
**(Permanent Retirement)** 978 1 4052 4805 1; £4.99

**Ben 10 chapter storybook 1**
**(And Then There Were 10/Kevin 11)** 978 1 4052 4467 1; £3.99

**Ben 10 chapter storybook 2**
**(The Alliance/Secrets)** 978 1 4052 4468 8; £3.99

**Ben 10 chapter storybook 3**
**(Truth/Framed)** 978 1 4052 4672 9; £4.99

**Ben 10 chapter storybook 4**
**(The Galactic Enforcers/Ultimate Weapon)** 978 1 4052 4673 6; £4.99

## *COMING SOON ...*
### *3 COOL NEW BEN 10 BOOKS!*

**Ben 10 Alien Force Extreme (Pop-Up)** 978 1 4052 4852 5; £14.99

**Ben 10 Alien Force chapter storybook 1**
**(All That Glitters/Max Out)** 978 1 4052 5006 1; £4.99

**Ben 10 Alien Force chapter storybook 2**
**(Paradox/Plumbers' Helpers)** 978 1 4052 5007 8; £4.99

# Visit Egmont.co.uk